THE STORY OF ANTIGONE

ALI SMITH

Illustrated by
Laura Paoletti

Pushkin Children's Books
71–75 Shelton Street
London WC2H 9JQ

The Story of Antigone first published in Italian as *La storia di Antigone*
© 2011 Gruppo Editoriale L'Espresso S.p.A
and © 2011 Ali Smith. All rights reserved.

First published in English by Pushkin Children's Books in 2013
This edition first published in 2015

ISBN 978 1 782690 89 4

Set in Garamond Premier Pro by Tetragon, London

Printed and bound in Italy by Printer Trento SRL
on Munken Print White 100gsm

www.pushkinpress.com

One

The crow crossed
the sky, slow-beating her
wings. Beat, beat, beat. It
was night, not yet morning,
and her feathers were so
black that she coasted the air
invisible above the city wall.

She upped her shoulders and angled her feet. She
landed on the gatepost and hopped into the nest.
There were seven gates altogether. This crow roosted
above the seventh, the best place to live, for a crow.
It had the best view of the battlefield.

The battle that had just ended had been by far
the foulest. Plenty to eat. It made her wish that right

now was the time of year she had a new-hatched batch of eggs; if only human beings could decide to kill each other at a more useful time of the year. But no, a whole season had passed since she'd nudged the broken eggshells out of the nest with her black beak and sent the slim young crows on their way.

Now what was left of the ships of the retreating army would be disappearing over the thin line where the sea met the sky; now the smoke of last night's fires was clearing where the still-alive humans below had buried and burnt their dead. They were mostly the female kind. The female kind did the sorting-out, afterwards. They worked their way through the rubble and the debris. Hunched and wingless, they wheeled their broken-yoked handcarts along what was left of the roads. It was nothing new. The crow had seen it all before. She was an old bird and the years had made her sharp-eyed and wise, had taught her how to know what to see and what to be blind to. And she knew not to spend too long choosing which good thing she'd like best to eat off a dead human left out on the ground. Never spend so long that any of the still-alive humans have the time to notice and find a stone and throw it. One: down. Two: land and grip with claws. Three: firm tug with beak at nose, finger, corner of tasty eye, strip of perfect supper. Four, quick: beat, beat, beat of the wings and up and out of there.

She rearranged her wing feathers with her beak. It had been a long night shift. She settled down ready to sleep.

But down below her, look, down by the gate, that dog was still sitting there, waiting.

He'd been there since the battle started.

"Caw!" she said.

The young dog turned wearily in the gravel and the dust once, then again. He was making a bed for himself.

His paws were big. He'd grow into the kind of dog you kept well out of the way of, the kind that'd take your whole tail off in one quick swipe, then sit there afterwards with your tail feathers sticking out of his mouth like a lady's fan (something like this had actually once happened to the crow). He was definitely dog, but close to wolf, sharp at the teeth and the ear, with a long and handsome muzzle.

He lay with his head on his paws. He looked miserable. But his ears were still cocked forwards. Some still-alive, probably dead, had told him: Stay. And he had.

"Go home. Your master's dead," the crow cawed down at the dog.

No response.

Dogs. They happily wore collars, let themselves be led around on bits of old rope by still-alive humans. They ate out of the hands of still-alive humans, as if the hand that fed them wasn't good food in itself.

"Probably burnt or buried already," she cawed.

Suddenly the dog leapt to his feet and when he did the crow's heart jumped. Beat, beat, beat! Even though there was no way that dog could jump as high as a city gate she threw herself up into the air, the feathers tingling at her tail.

But that dog didn't notice. Instead, he stood listening, one paw lifted in the air.

The little door in the huge wooden gate opened.

Through it came two still-alive human girls. They came warily, as if they were guarding a secret.

Two

The two girls were too young to be out of the city and wandering the edge of this blasted landscape by themselves. They were well dressed, not at all the kind of girl you usually saw sneaking around the city wall at dawn.

One was about twelve human years old. The other was maybe a little older, though they looked very alike (well, all still-alive humans did). But they were acting very differently. The younger one was forging forwards and the older one was pulling back.

"Because we're *sisters*," the younger one was saying. "Because of us being the same *blood*."

The more she talked, the more the older one, her sister, looked scared, looked around her, looked like she wished with all her heart that the younger one would be quieter.

"And now this," the louder girl said. "Food for crows."

The old crow sat up in her nest. Food? Specifically for crows?

"Antigone," the older girl said. "I don't know what you're talking about."

"Listen better, Ismene," the younger one said.

Now the old crow really sat up and took notice. Antigone and Ismene! The little princesses! Here below the nest was all that was left of King Oedipus's family, the old human royal family.

Well well. Princess Antigone. She'd been the one who was so kind to Oedipus, the blind man. The man who'd once been king. Her father. She'd been her father's eyes, that girl, till he died (after which point, of course, eyes are nothing *but* food specifically for crows).

The crow had seen them, the small girl leading the ruined man in his torn royal robes, many's the time out on the road.

"Shh, Antigone!" her sister said. "All I know is,

they're both dead now too. Our brothers. Eteocles and Polynices. Killed by each other. In the same instant. That's all I know."

She stood there, fragile as a long piece of grass. She had very nice hair, the crow thought, good for crow nest-lining. Beside her, her little sister burned like a lit torch in the dull grey air.

"Listen," she said. "*Creon says* one of our brothers is a hero and the other is a traitor. *Creon says* poor dead Eteocles is the hero. *Creon says* poor dead Eteocles is to be buried with honours, a brass band, a twenty-one-gun salute."

"Yes," Ismene said and wiped at one of her eyes. "Poor Eteocles."

"But *Creon also says* poor dead Polynices is a traitor," Antigone said. "*Creon also says* that because he's a traitor he has to be left unburied. *Creon also says* nobody is allowed to cover him up. Or say prayers. Or ask for him to be welcomed in the underworld. Or even to feel sad, or show any sadness at all. And if anyone tries to bury him, then *Creon also says* that this 'anyone' will be stoned to death in the city."

Stoned to death, the crow thought. Caw.

"And it's *our brother* he's talking about," Antigone said, "lying unburied in the open air. Unburied treasure. Treasure for crows, more like."

Now there's a girl who understands things, the crow thought.

She got ready to set out as soon as the little one said where this good dead body was.

"So, Ismene," Antigone said. "Here it is."

"Here what is?" Ismene said.

"Here's your chance," Antigone said and took her sister's hand.

"How do you mean, my chance?" Ismene said.

She pulled her hand away. She backed away from her sister. Her sister came forwards and held out her hand again. From the crow's nest it was like watching a dance the sisters knew the steps of already, a dance they'd done a hundred times.

"Your chance to show me how noble you are," Antigone said. "Worthy, illustrious, real royalty. To show me what you're made of."

"Me?" Ismene said.

"What *we're* made of," Antigone said.

"You look like a wild animal!" her sister said. "Don't look at me like that."

"Come on," the younger girl said. "You and me. We'll lift him up. We'll bury our poor dead Polynices."

"You mean break the law?" Ismene said.

Stoned to death if they do, the crow thought.

"He's my brother," Antigone said. "When exactly did he stop being yours?"

"The law," Ismene said. "Don't be stupid, Antigone. The King says."

Antigone crossed her arms. "The King can't tell me what's right and what's wrong when it comes to me and my brother," she said.

"But the scandal!" Ismene said. "And think about what happened to our dad."

Antigone's eyes filled with tears.

"Think about what happened to our mum," Ismene said.

"I do," Antigone said. "I think about it all the time."

Caw. It was true. The crow had forgotten about that. These still-alive girls down there had no one else in the world.

"What if we were both gone in the blink of an eye too?" Ismene said. "What use would that be? And what can we do anyway? We're not even properly royal any more. We're underlings. Worse, we're underlings *and* we're women. We're not meant to even be outside the city *walls*, never mind be squaring up to our uncle. To a king. To politics. To the law."

The little one nodded. She turned her back on her sister.

"I'll do it myself," she said.

"Antigone," her sister said. "They'll kill you."

"I've got to die anyway," Antigone said, still with her back turned. "I've got to be dead for a lot longer than I'm going to be alive."

"You're mad," her sister said. "And you're scaring me. But I promise. I won't tell anybody what you're going to do."

That made the littler sister turn round and face her older sister again.

"SHOUT IT AS LOUD AS YOUR VOICE WILL GO!" she shouted. "I DON'T CARE WHAT YOU SAY. I DON'T CARE WHAT *CREON SAYS.* I DON'T CARE WHAT ANYONE SAYS."

Three

Off she went. The crow watched
her go. She was burning hot, that
child, and cool as a cucumber at the
same time.

Her sister stood, her arms hanging by her sides,
hopeless. She turned and saw the dog there at the
wall. The dog looked back at her with big, soulful
eyes. Then they both watched Antigone disappear
through the battle ruins and head off towards the
wilderness.

"Mad as she is," she said. "The best. The finest
sister in the world."

Then the pretty young still-alive human patted
the dog on the head and slipped back into the city
through the door in the big wooden gate.

The still-alives. They were all crazy.

The crow went to put her head beneath her wing,
when that dog below started up. What a noise.

AroooOOOOooo. WharrooOOoOOoo.

Dogs. Stupid *and* sentimental. She straightened a
wing feather. *And* hypocrites. They'll take a bite out
of a dead body any day, if they're hungry or greedy

enough. If there happens to be a body lying around. If nobody happens to have fed the poor darling his sweetened milk and his biscuits.

Ah, but he was just a pup, after all. He didn't know the history. How could he, just six months old?

And think of that little girl, just a pup herself she'd been, out on the road with the blind man, her father.

Think how she led him through rivers that came as deep as her chest, through storms, into shade when it was too hot, saw him safely through thieves and kindnesses.

It was enough to move the heart of even an old, tough-hearted, worldly-wise black crow.

The crow hopped to the edge of the nest. She took to the air. Beat, beat, beat.

She swooped up, then down. She landed on the ground at a safe distance from the dog. She drew a line in the dust with her beak.

"I'll tell you the whole story if you swear not to cross it," she said.

"Arf," the dog said and wagged his tail.

"Sit," the crow said.

The dog sat.

"Lie down," the crow said.

The dog lay down.

"Play dead," the crow said.

The dog rolled over onto his back, paws in the air.

Cretin, the crow thought.

"Good doggie," she said.

The dog panted and smiled, rolled back over onto his front. The smile revealed his teeth.

The crow hopped back a little further.

"History lesson number one," she said.

"Arf," the dog said.

"Those two girls are the daughters of the old king, King Oedipus, have you heard of him?" the crow said. "No? When his name's been more in the mouths of the still-alive people in the city than food itself?"

"Arf," the dog said.

His tongue lolled out of his mouth.

"Well," she said. "First he was a great hero here, Oedipus. He was a young, handsome stranger who arrived in the nick of time and saved this city from the monster. The Sphinx. Have you heard of the Sphinx? Like a really frightening, giant sort of cat?"

The dog growled.

"Anyway, it's Oedipus who got rid of it," the crow said.

"Bow how?" the dog said.

"That's too long a story to go into here," the crow said. "The thing is, he did. And because he did, he got to become the king and marry the queen, whose husband, the old king, had died mysteriously in a fight at a crossroads with, listen, a *young, handsome stranger*."

The dog looked confused. The crow ignored this.

"Because, listen, this Oedipus," she went on, "he'd been cursed at birth, and the curse was that he'd kill his father and marry his mother."

The dog shrugged.

"I know," the crow said. "Makes no difference to me either. But it's the kind of rubbish that preoccupies the still-alives. Scandal. Fate. Gods. Curses. They wear them like clothes. It's because they've no feathers. Or fur."

"Arf," the dog said.

"Anyway," the crow continued. "When his father and mother heard about the curse, that their lovely little baby would one day kill one of them and marry the other, they had their lovely little baby taken out and left on a hillside for the crows to eat. And to make sure he'd not be able to go far on the hillside, escape his fate, they pierced his feet. That's why his name was Oedipus, which means big, swollen feet. Even bigger than yours, caw."

The dog looked down at his own paws. Then he started chewing at one of them. Then he had a look at his other front paw and started chewing at it instead. The crow sighed.

"Listen!" she said. "No crows ate him. He survived, and grew up, and then managed to kill his father at a crossroads without knowing the man was his father, then marry his own mother without knowing she was his mother! Caw. Hilarious."

The dog's eyes were big and round.

"So," the crow said. "What happened then was this. First his mother/wife killed herself, didn't she, for 'shame'. For 'scandal'. And what did King Oedipus do then, for goodness sake? He put his hands inside his own head and he took out his own eyes! And off he went, wandering the world like an old tramp, not a king at all. And then when he died, what happened? Typical still-alive stuff. His two sons, the big brothers of those two girls we just saw arguing, decided they'd share being king instead. Then guess what happened. Go on. Guess."

The young dog looked bewildered.

"Caw! So slow! You're no crow," the old crow said.

She told the dog that when it came to the time for the first brother to stop being king, he simply said no. And that's what the battle had been about. The other brother had formed an army and this army had attacked the city. Loads of still-alives had died in the fight, including the two brothers themselves. In fact, the story went that the one who was the king had run his sword through his brother at exactly the same moment as his brother did it back to him. Priceless. Anyway, after all that, now their uncle was the brand-new king. Creon, that was his name.

"Still-alives." The crow shook her feathers in disgust. "They fought. They died. And all along the way they made up dreadful poetry about themselves."

Right then, as if on cue, out of the gate came the fifteen ancient Elders of Thebes, with their robes and their long beards swaying in the early morning heat haze.

"Caw," the crow said, and rose into the air.

Beat, beat, beat.

She settled into her nest and put one wing over her head. The Elders always sent her very nicely to sleep.

Four

Fifteen very old men arranged themselves in a semicircle. They fell over their own feet. They argued a bit amongst themselves.

Then, out of nowhere, they all started singing in unison.

"How lovely it is to see it, the sun. Now that the terrible battle we've won!

War flew over the city like a great big bird. It was because of Polynices that it occurred.

And for the whole time of the fighting none of us could rhyme. Which was making us all go crazy and should be classed as a capital crime.

But thank Zeus, who knows that a lack of verse really frightening for us is. He went and knocked them off their horses with true poetic justice.

And now the new king Creon is coming to greet the new day. He wants to make a speech to us and we're wondering what he'll say.

But hurray for us! War's over! There'll be dancing in the temples! Because... Because..."

Then they all stopped.

The eldest, wisest and most wrinkled Elder stood and stroked at his longest-of-all beard and went through the alphabet, counting words off on his bony fingers.

"*Bemples, demples, femples, gemples, hemples, jemples...*" he said.

"*Pimples?*" someone said at the back.

All fifteen of them thought about it. Then all fifteen of them shook their heads in unison.

Just then a trumpet blew from high on the city walls. It woke the crow and made several of the Elders below drop their walking sticks.

The great gate opened for the first time since the beginning of the war.

The youngest of the fifteen, who was ninety-seven, bent to pick up his stick, shook it in the air to catch the attention of the others, and proclaimed:

"*We'll have to decide on the rhyme for temples later. Because here comes the new king, now, look, through the seventh city gate-r.*"

Everybody applauded the youngest Elder. The King, on his horse, thought they were applauding him. He bowed regally. Then he started to speak.

The Elders listened as keenly as old deaf men can.

"Gracious Elders of Thebes!" the new king said. "The good ship of our city is safe on calm waters again!"

Ooh, the crow thought. The old safe ship metaphor. They wheel it out every time, the new kings.

"We've come safely through the storm, and now I'm the king," King Creon said. "And I've called you here before me today because I know your loyalty. You were loyal to King Eteocles. You were loyal, before him, to King Oedipus. You were loyal, before him, to the king before him and the king before him, and the king before him and the, eh, king before him. Now you'll be loyal to me."

All the Elders nodded.

"Because it's only when the city is as safe as houses," the King said, "only when the ship is shipshape that we're any good in the world as a power. And that's how I intend to make us a world power. I intend to make us great."

Everybody nodded.

"Now," the King said. "Just one little thing to add. We all know the late King Eteocles was a hero. He died defending us, and I'm going to have a statue put up to him right here at the gate, as befits a national hero. But his brother, Polynices, is a traitor. Eteocles was a hero. Polynices is a zero."

Much nodding happened.

"And I'm ruling," the King said, "once and for all, today, right here and right now, that nobody, and I mean nobody, is to remember Polynices. Because Polynices is—a nobody. And nobody is to touch his dead body. He's to be left to rot where he fell and died, out in the open air, and dogs, like that one there sitting at the gate, and the crows, like that one up there in that nest, can have his dead body, rip it to pieces, make a stew of what's left of him, bones, brains, muscles, liver, lights."

The Elders looked startled.

"Now, is that understood?" the King said. "Because whoever is loyal to the city is honourable. And whoever isn't loyal to the city is worth nothing. Crow stew. Everybody got that?"

"*Your Highness, we agree with everything you said. You're the king of the living and the king of the dead,*" the Elders said.

"A still-alive king thinks he's king of the dead, caw-haw!" the old crow cawed.

"*Your Highness, you're the king, at the end of the day. And that's why we'll all do exactly what you say.*"

"Yes," King Creon said. "Thank you. Which is why I want you Elders gathered here today to make sure my orders are carried out about nobody touching this dead body I'm talking about."

The Elders panicked.

"*Us? Oh no! We're far far far too old! We can hardly stand, never mind be made to guard a horrible dead body in the heat and in the cold!*"

"No, no," King Creon said. "That's not what I mean. Obviously I've got guards watching the body. What I mean is, just make sure none of you Gracious Theban Elders find yourselves supporting anyone who goes against my decree."

"*Against your decree? Not us! Not us! We know you'll execute anyone who does!*" the Elders said.

"I know you're loyal," King Creon said. "I know you're wise. But there's always bribery."

The crow saw the King's eye twitch like the eye of a magpie twitched when it saw a shiny thing.

"I'm no fool. People will do all sorts of things for a handful of gold. Won't they?" the King said.

Just then, a ragged, dusty-looking man appeared

on the brow of the battle ruins. He came forwards, but then he stepped back as if he'd changed his mind. Then he thought the better of it and came forwards again.

He was a guard, in guard's uniform.

"Your Highness," he said. "I've just come all the way to tell you. And I didn't really want to, but I did it anyway, see? Which just lets you know what kind of chap I am. And I came as fast as I could. Well, I mean, I ran a bit, and then I stopped and had a think."

"Who is this man?" the King said.

"But it was a quick think," the guard said. "Well, granted, I'm not that quick a thinker, but I'm not totally slow. And there was a lot to think about, which is why I wasn't here sooner."

"What's he talking about?" the King said.

"Anyway. Here I am," the guard said. "And it wasn't me!"

He turned and ran three or four steps away. Then he stopped and turned round again.

"What wasn't you?" the King said.

"Any of it!" the guard said. "And I didn't see who did do it, either, see? None of us saw. But then I drew the, what's it called? The short straw. Which is why I'm the one who has to come and tell you, and everyone else is getting off scot-free but me."

"Tell me WHAT?" King Creon shouted.

He slid off his horse and got the guard by the chainmail at the back of his neck.

"What we didn't see, see?" the guard said. "And what we didn't see was... the someone who tried to... you know... bury it."

"Bury WHAT?" the King hollered.

He dashed the guard to the ground.

"The dead man you told us to guard," the guard said. "When we looked. Someone had covered him, with a little bit of earth, not much."

The King shook his head. The crown on his head shook wildly as he did.

"A wild animal, maybe," the King said. "Scraping the dust round it. Was that it?"

"Well," the guard said. "To be blunt. No. The thing is, Your Highness. It was a bit what you'd call neat for an animal. And someone had also done that thing where you pour out wine on the ground, what's the word, ritual, you know, to honour them, the dead. We could smell it, the wine. But we didn't see any, wine I mean. Or drink any. We didn't see or drink anything. I swear."

Five

That's when the King went crazy. He hauled the guard off the ground and shook him like a dog shakes a rabbit.

"Someone has paid you to do this," he yelled. "You are in the pay of my enemies."

"With re-e-spect," the guard said between shakes, "Yo-o-ur Hi-i-ghness, but you're to-o-tally wrong about tha-at."

"Then I'm holding you responsible," the King said most menacingly. "So *you'd better* find who did this or I'll string *you—and your friends—*up as an example."

He dropped the guard into the dust again.

"Now that's *really* unfair," the guard said.

But luckily for him the King didn't hear him. He was back up on his horse and off. The gate opened to let him in, then swung shut after him.

The guard stood up and dusted himself down.

"Phew!" he said.

He wiped at his elbows and his knees. He strapped back on the metal sheaths that he'd had on his arms to protect them, and which had both fallen off when the King shook him so fiercely.

"Now, correct me if I'm wrong, but I was under the impression he's meant to be our new king, not our new tyrant. Well, that's the last you'll see of me," he said to the quaking Elders.

Off he went.

The Elders rearranged their robes. Then they formed their semicircle.

"Man is a wonder, a wonder of worth.
He sails the wide sea and he ploughs the wide earth.
He tames the wild birds and he catches
the fishes.
He makes all the animals do what he wishes.
He's made up a language for all that he'll say.
His houses and cities keep winter at bay.
If he's ill he can make himself well really fast.
It's just death itself that he can't quite get past.
He lives by the laws, if the laws aren't evil.
He goes to the good or he goes to the devil.
He's tall and he's noble, or low and a louse.
And I know which of those I won't let in my house."

The crow up in the nest shook herself awake.

Then the eldest Elder whistled for the dog. The dog got up, shook his coat, wagged his tail. He lolloped over from the wall. The Elders fussed over him, scruffed his neck and chest. He sat in the middle of them all with his ears back, friendly.

"Caw-haw!" said the crow above. "I'd like to see any man try and tame *me*."

But the dog began to bark. A cloud of dust had risen on the path. Yes, a clump of soldiers was coming over the hill, leading a small girl in chains.

"What is this? This cannot be! Arrested! Little Antigone!"

Uh oh. Here we go, thought the crow.

Then she shook her feathers in disgust. Rhyme. Uch. A lot of the things that the still-alives did were catching.

The guard at the front was the man who'd been here a moment ago. "Where's the King now, then?" he was shouting. "Where's a king when you need one to see that you're innocent and not guilty and that it wasn't you who did it?"

The great gate opened. There was Creon, high on his horse.

"Who calls on the King in such a rude fashion?" he bellowed.

The guard pushed the still-alive girl in the chains until she was right in front of the King.

"See?" he said.

"Why is my niece under arrest?" the King said.

A worried murmur went round the guards. The King's niece. Uh oh.

"Burying," the guard said. "Body."

"You're lying," the King said.

"What, you think I'm a fool as well as a guard in your armed forces?" the guard said. "Here's the truth, the whole truth and nothing but the truth so help me God. See, first you threatened to hang me, then hang us all. So I went back and told my fellow guardsmen. And we went over to that body, and we brushed it till there was no dust and earth on it, see? But then, you know, the smell of it, it was a bit strong, with the heat and all. So we all went and sat upwind.

"And then the wind got stronger and stronger, and an awful storm came out of nowhere, and dust and leaves blew up into the air and into our eyes and we couldn't see anything. But we could hear an awful shrieking, like a bird that gets back to its nest and finds its eggs are gone.

"And when the storm calmed down and we could see again, what we saw was... her. She was scattering earth from its head to its foot. And when we got to her, she was pouring water and wine into the ground. So we stopped her. And brought her. And did what you said. So you've to pardon me right now, eh, Your Majesty. And my friends. With respect, and all. Because I didn't. We didn't. Do it. See?"

The King got off his horse.

The girl was so small she didn't even come up to his chest.

"Did you?" he said.

Antigone looked up, right at him, in the eyes.

"I'm denying nothing," she said.

"And you knew about the penalty?" the King said.

"Everyone knows," Antigone said.

"And you broke the law all the same?" the King said.

"You're not a god," Antigone said. "What you say doesn't go when it comes to the dead. I'm happy to die for my dead brother. He was my mother's son. I'm my mother's daughter."

The eldest of the Elders stepped forwards and crossed the waste ground. He was shaking, but he placed himself between the girl and the King.

"*Think about the mother. Don't forget the dad. It wouldn't be her fault, now, if she acts a little mad,*" he said quietly.

Then he took a respectful step back.

Creon nodded to himself.

"There are wild horses," he said, "and they're easy to tame. All you need is a little piece of metal, about this size. All you do is put it in their mouths."

He held up his hand, measured four or five inches in the air with his finger and thumb.

"She's guilty," he said. "She will suffer the most terrible of deaths. Oh yes. And her sister too. Her sister's every bit as guilty and will suffer the most terrible of deaths too."

"*What? What? No she's not!*" the Elders whispered.

"What sister?" the soldiers whispered.

"How many deaths do you need?" the small girl said to the King. "Everyone here knows you're wrong. They're just too scared to tell you."

She looked round at all the other still-alives.

"Aren't you?" she said.

Silence.

"Well, you'll be quiet too, soon," the King said. "I think you'll enjoy being dead, since you love the dead so much. And you forget. He was a traitor, your brother."

"He was my brother, your traitor," the girl said. "It's not me who's forgetting."

Six

Right then Ismene came through the open city gate. She cried out when she saw the chains round her sister's hands. She bent and tore a piece of soft pink material off her own pretty dress, then wound it round Antigone's wrist, under the chain, so the chain wouldn't chafe.

"Ah!" the King said. "The sister-snake. The snake-sister. So. Tell me the truth. You did this too, didn't you?"

"Yes," Ismene said. "I did."

Antigone snatched her hand away. She shook her arm until the piece of torn dress wafted out from between her skin and the metal chain.

"You did not," she said.

The piece of torn dress fell and settled on the ground.

"I am equally to blame," Ismene said.

She put her arm round Antigone. Antigone shook her off.

"She's got no right to say this," Antigone shouted. "She's done nothing heroic. Not like me."

This made the old crow sit up in her nest. This was good and complicated. Was the little one really

so arrogant? Or was she maybe trying to protect her sister, so her sister wouldn't die?

"You chose life," the little one said. "It's me who chose death."

"What's the point of me being alive if you're dead?" the sister said.

"You're both as good as dead already," the King said with a laugh.

But all the same, he hasn't ordered the guards to seize that sister, thought the crow. He doesn't dare.

"And you, Uncle Creon," Ismene said. "You'd kill her. My sister. Your niece. Even though you know your son, your only son, is so in love with her? Even though the date is set for their wedding and everything?"

This was news! The crow liked a royal wedding. There was always lots of good garbage after a royal wedding.

"My son Haemon, marry a criminal? Marry someone who's gone against my word? Over my dead body—or his own," the King said.

All the same, he'd looked a little unsteady. He'd looked it since the little girl had told him that everybody secretly agreed with her. He looked even unsteadier now, faced with both girls like this.

"Take these women inside," he said suddenly, turning away, waving a hand in the air. "Women. They should've been inside all along."

Off went the soldiers and the two girls, one in chains, one going freely by her side.

The King suddenly looked decidedly weary.

With their eyes shut, the Elders sang this song at him.

"*It's good if we live without going to the bad. For the gods can take all that we have or we had. The gods are as broad as an ocean, as high. As a sea storm that rears up the size of a sky. And us in a ship that's as small as a fly. That's the way the gods deal with us, before we die.*

*The gods are much bigger than men, as we say. And
no human can magic their power away. And when a
man gets any power at all. Then his road to disaster's
inevitable. Far better be small and be quiet, we say.
Than to live out your life the disastrous way."*

The dog came and put his nose into the King's
hand. The King looked down, saw the dog, took his
hand away immediately and wiped it on his robe.

Seven

*"Here's your son, Your Majesty, arrived
to find out what. Is happening and
whether he'll be married soon or not. He's
promised to Antigone but now his little
one. Is promised to the crows and dogs
instead of to your son."*

"Your rhyming is appalling," the King said.

*"Your Majesty is always right and never ever
wrong. We'll always back Your Majesty, however poor
our song,"* the Elders sang.

Sure enough, here came young Haemon.

"Well, son?" the King said. "Come to argue with
me, have you? Angry, are you?"

But the boy looked calm, as if he were simply
returning from a nice stroll along the sunlit road
through the battle ruins.

"You're my father," he said.

He knelt down and bowed his head.

"I'll always do what you say," he said, "and I'll
always trust that you're right."

The King drew himself up to his full height.

"Now, that's what I call a son," he said. "Exactly the kind of son every man prays for. A son who'd never be stupid enough to think more of a mere woman than he does of his dad."

The Elders bowed their heads too.

"*Yes! Yes! Very wise! We are leaving shut our eyes,*" they sang.

"Yes, she can go and, shall we say, *wed the dead,* eh, son, am I right?" the King said. "The only person in this whole city to go against what I said. I'd treat all family the same way. All really excellent kings and rulers would. Am I right? And I'm relieved it's gone this way, son. Because it would've looked especially bad if I'd been defeated by a woman. Not even a woman, just a girl. Right, son?"

Haemon shook his head.

"You're right, father," he said. "But it's also possible that there are other ways to see this, and that those other ways are right too."

"I'm sorry?" Creon said.

"The whole city," his son said. "In mourning. Not for the body, but for the girl. *Just a girl.*"

"Come again?" Creon said.

"Nobody's brave enough to say it to you," Haemon said. "But they think she's right not to want her brother to be eaten by dogs and birds. That's what's being said, all over the city, under everyone's breath. So maybe, father, it's important to see more than one side of this argument."

"I don't think I'm hearing you quite right," Creon said.

"Like a tree," Haemon said, "in a storm. It has to be able to bend, or it'll snap. Like a ship whose sail is too tightly bound. It'll capsize, in a storm, unless it's loosened."

"*Yes, yes! Very wise! Dare we open up our eyes?*" the Elders sang.

"We should all open up our eyes," the boy said.

"Told what to do, me?" the King said. "By a pup? Me? The King? Dictated to by nothing but mere citizens?"

"I'm saying it for the good of you, me, her, all the citizens, and I'm saying it for the gods too," his son said.

The King stamped his foot.

"You'll never marry her alive," he said.

"Well," his son said, calm as anything. "I'll marry her dead, then. Because if you kill her, her death will breed."

"Are you threatening me?" the King bellowed.

"What I'm saying," his son said, "is this. I'll see her dead and I'll see you in hell."

Off he went. He left his father speechless.

"What on earth are you going to do? What if it all goes wrong for you?"

"It won't," the King said. "Both those girls. Going to. Die. And that's my final word on it."

The semicircle of Elders took a step forwards.

"Are you sure it's the proven truth? Are you sure you should kill them both?"

"Hmm," the King said.

He took a step back from the Elders.

"I take your point," he said. "Maybe you're right. OK. Just the one, then. We'll just kill the littler one."

The Elders, in unison, took another step forwards.

"*So many people thinking that she's right. D'you think it's wise to kill her, quite?*"

"Hmm," the King said.

He swivelled on the spot.

"I take your point" he said. "Maybe you're right."

He thought about it for a moment. Then he snapped his fingers.

"How about... since she wanted to bury her dead brother so badly. How about... since she's so in love with burial. How about... we bury *her*? Alive, I mean? How about I have her taken to that old cave near the border and, you know, leave her some food, a little food for good measure, and then wall up the mouth of the cave? And then it's not exactly like I'm killing her, is it? How about that?"

Off he went the opposite way from his son, in great excitement.

The Elders sang:

"Love doesn't care about money, love is much hotter than heat. Whether the war's lost or won, it's love that'll never be beat. Love has no rhyme or no reason, love makes sane people go mad. Love is as wide as all seas, and it's bigger than Mum or than Dad. Love wins all games and all wars, fought here or below or above. Nothing's as forceful a source, not anything, nothing, like love."

Eight

But they stopped singing when
they saw her being led out by the
soldiers, the little still-alive, Antigone.

She was ragged and pale.

"Look," she said. "The sun on my chains. Look
how it glints. The sun, on me, for the last time."

The Elders shuffled up to her as if to console.

"*The folk will say you never suffered illness. The folk
will say how healthfully you died. The folk will say you
never got decrepit. How lucky you are! Look on the
bright side!*"

On the bright side!

The King galloped his horse to the front of
the procession.

"See? I'm not responsible," he said. "It's not
my doing, when she dies."

Then Antigone spoke, like a wine glass would
speak, or a water glass, if a piece of shaped glass
could speak.

"I had no more brothers than Eteocles and you,
Polynices," she said out loud to her dead brother.
"There was nothing else for me to do. And now I'll

never have a husband. I'll never have children. Well. If the gods think it's fair, this chain of events…"

She held up her chained hands in the sunlight.

"Then fair enough. But if they don't, I wish exactly what's happened to me will happen back to those who are doing this to me."

The procession set off again. When it reached the brow of the hill and was about to disappear from sight, the dog jumped up and scurried after it.

The Elders sang their most ridiculous song yet, about an imprisoned princess who couldn't escape fate, and then about a violent man who realized he'd been wrong but still, yes, couldn't escape fate. Whatever happened in it, nobody could escape fate. Caw! The Fates were to blame for everything, were they? Caw. The songs of the still-alives.

The crow rose from the nest. Beat, beat, beat. She soared in an arc, first up, then down. She landed at the feet of the singers blinding themselves with their own song, and she snatched up the piece of pink fabric that the sister had torn off her dress.

She took to the air again
with it firmly in her beak. Not a single
Elder noticed. Beat, beat, beat.
    The piece of torn stuff would make
    very good nest-lining.

Nine

She wove it into the nest, between twigs and a hardened piece of moss. When she'd finished doing this, the King and his retinue were coming marching back to the city, the same procession, except there was no little still-alive girl at the front of it. The law had been carried out.

But what was that huge black cloud above them? It looked like—it sounded like—a furious cloud of crows.

Beat, beat, beat. The old crow made her way towards the sight.

The Elders struggled up the hill towards it too.

She landed in the burnt branches of a tree. The King's whole retinue was being held at a standstill on the road by an old, old man. His back was straighter than any old man's ever could be. He was dressed in clothes so white you had to look away. By his side, holding his hand, was a small boy.

That, and the magical whiteness of his clothes, signalled who the beautiful old man was.

Tiresias, the crow thought to herself.

Every creature alive knew Tiresias. He was a shape-shifter; he had been both human male and human female in his time, so it was told. He was blind, as blind as the old king. But his blindness was different; it meant he was able to see, and what he could see instead was the future. Because of this, the still-alive humans respected his powers and came to him for advice. Also, the animals loved him. The luckiest crows in the world were the ones who got to sit on his shoulder.

And now Creon was looking down from the height of his horse at the old, old man. He held his

hand over his eyes in a slant because of the light that came from Tiresias. He also had on his face what could only be described as a sneer.

"I'm going to pretend you didn't say any of that," the King said. "And I'm going to continue on my way. You've been good in the past, Tiresias, I admit. But this proves you've lost it. You've lost it, old man."

The guards cringed.

The Elders looked stricken with worry.

"But I know, King Creon, because of my birds," Tiresias said.

He held out his blind hand and the crow knew what she was meant to do.

Beat, beat, beat.

She flew from the tree and landed on the fine old hand. There she sat, black against the glow of the white.

"My birds went mad," Tiresias said. "I heard them above me. They were making a terrible noise. Then I heard the ripping of wings and feathers. They were tearing each other apart. So I checked my sacred fire, where I leave my daily gift to the gods, to ask them to keep things right and kind here on earth. And I asked my boy here, my guide, what he saw, and he said that instead of a fire there was a waxen, fatty liquid resembling a tongue more than a flame. It is a terrible sign, King Creon. And on my way here I passed the carcasses of many of my faithful dogs, and every so often one of the crazed birds would fall down dead out of the sky. It was because they had eaten it."

"Eaten what, you old fool?" the King said.

"The body," Tiresias said. "King Creon, you can't kill a dead man. A dead man is already dead. It is not yet too late, if you listen."

"Who has bribed you all to turn against me?" the King yelled in fury.

Tiresias, calm, blinked his blank white eyes. He let go of the boy's hand. He felt for the crow and stroked her feathers as he said this:

"Then what I see is this, King Creon. Your own heirs will die. Your own house will be empty of everything but mourning. All the torn things of the world will compare their tornness to you. You will be nobody."

Then he moved his hand

gently, decisively, so that the crow flew off and settled back on the branch of the tree.

The guards stepped aside and Tiresias, with the small boy leading him by the hand, went silently on his way.

Behind him walked the young dog, with his head bent and his tail down.

Tiresias's dog. Well well!

"Oh god," the King said. He covered his face with his hands.

The Elders semicircled round him.

"Your Highness, it's Tiresias. Your Highness, we implore. If we were you, Your Majesty, his words we'd not ignore."

It was as if the blinding light coming off Tiresias had whitewashed the King's face.

When he spoke his voice was very small.

"What do you think I should do?" he said.

The Elders' response was instant.

"Let the girl out of the cave.

Take away the rocks.

Get her out of there then put that body in a box.

Take the rocks away.

Unblock the entrance to that cave.

Get the girl out.
Burn the dead man.
Put him in a grave."
"You think so?" the King wavered.
The Elders shouted like madmen.
"*Girl out!*
No rocks!
Body in a clean box!
Rocks away!
Open cave!
Burn body!
Quick! Grave!"
"It's hard, to be defeated," the King said.

Finally he gently nudged his horse forwards. He went slowly, then it was as if he woke himself up. He spurred his horse. Guards ran after him. Dust rose on the road.

Epilogue

"Tell us again! Tell us again!" It was
another dawn. It was nearly a year later.
The nest was full of hungry fledglings
still wet from the egg, who'd all woken
with their hungry mouths (and ears)
wide open.

The old crow was doling out the night's worth of
scraps.

"Tell us again about Antipode!" the littlest one cried.

"Antigone," the old crow said.

"Antigone!" the littlest one said.

This littlest crow would have the hardest time surviving, she was so small.

"Start with the best bit, the bit with all those bodies piled up at the end," the biggest one said.

That biggest one would have no problem at all surviving. He already ate the eagle's share of the food.

"Well, I will," the old crow said, "if you'll all quieten down and listen."

Squealing stopped. Their mouths stayed open, but no sounds came out.

"Good," the old crow said. "Well, what happened at the end was this."

"A fantastic pile-up of food!" the fledglings shouted.

"Because first the King went with his guards to bury the dead brother, and maybe he should have gone to the cave first and let the girl out!" the littlest one said.

"But he didn't," the old crow said, "that's right.

He went and dealt with the dead instead of the
still-alive. So by the time he and his guards had
done all the things still-alives do to honour their
dead, then gone afterwards to the cave, what had
happened?"

"The still-alive girl, Antigone, was dead too!" the
crow babies squealed.

"Yes," the old crow said. "She'd decided she'd
end her life by herself, then and there in the cave,
because she was so sad that she'd never see the sun
again. Among other things. But her lover, the King's
son, got into the cave to try and stop her."

"Too late!" one of the fledglings shouted.

"Yes," the old crow said. "His true love was
already dead. And he was crying and crying, and his
father and the guards removed all the heavy rocks
from the mouth of the cave and the King heard his
son, and ran to comfort him. And the son drew his
sword and very nearly killed the King, his father.
But then what happened?"

"Instead," the largest fledgling said, "he used the
sword on himself, and soon he was dead too. And
that wasn't all. Because then the news of the boy
dying got back to his mother, the King's wife, back

at the palace in the city, who loved her son, didn't she, and she was so upset that she killed herself too. And they all died happily ever after."

"All died happily ever after!" all the fledglings cawed.

"A very happy ending," the littlest one said.

"A happy ending for crows," their mother, the old crow, said.

"Tell us again. Tell us from the start," they cawed.

They liked stories even better than worms.

"Tell us again the story of the still-alive girl who cared about her dead brother," cawed the first.

"The story of the girl who broke the law," cawed the next.

"The story of the king who wanted to make his city great," cawed the next.

"The story of the lovely long-eared dog," the littlest one said.

The littlest one was going to have trouble surviving, being so sentimental.

"Tell us again the story about: the mad black cloud of crows/the tasty body/the time our own mother sat on the hand of the wise Tiresias/the brave still-alive boy who stood up to his father/the piece of pink material that got woven into our nest," cawed the next and the next and the next.

That piece of pink stuff lined the nest, all right. But so, somehow, did all the stories they asked so hungrily for, the old crow thought to herself.

Then, because it was dawn, down below the nest the small door opened in the great gate. Out stumbled the fifteen elderly Elders of Thebes. They fell over each other's feet. They fell over their own sticks, and tripped on their own beards. They stood in their semicircle and they began again, like every day.

"How lovely it is, to see it, the sun. To know that another fine day has begun.

The older we get, we hope we get wiser. The more we find out what the hows and the whys are.

Respect to the gods when the sun starts to rise. All the way to the night and the closing of eyes.

The older we are, the more that we'll know. And we'll do our best between dog, man and crow."

The old crow looked at her fledglings. It never failed. Completely asleep, every one of them. But they'd be awake and open-mouthed again in the blink of a bird's eye. Nothing was more certain.

She'd need to be teaching them how to stay awake and alert soon. And then how to fly.

And then, most important of all, how to find food.

Off she went in search of it herself.

Beat, beat, beat.

This book is dedicated to our daughter Helen, with love.

WHERE IS THIS
STORY FROM?

(An interview, with Crow and Ali Smith)

CROW: So, where does the story of
Antigone come from?

ALI: Antigone is a character from
Greek mythology. One of the most famous and most
memorable ways her story has been told and retold
over the many centuries, and one of the reasons the
story has lasted and has kept being told over and
over again all this time, is that there's a brilliant play
about her, a Greek tragedy written by Sophocles in
or around the year 442 BC. Sophocles was a very
renowned Greek playwright (also a general in the
Greek army) who wrote over 100 plays. Most of his
plays are lost now. Only seven of them survived, and
one of these is *Antigone*. It's one of three plays now
known as the Theban Plays; the other two are about
Oedipus, Antigone's father, and are called *Oedipus
at Colonus* and *Oedipus the King*. *Antigone* seems

to have been the earliest written of these plays, even though the things which happen in it take place after the events which happen in the other two.

It's clear that Sophocles was very interested in the character of Antigone. Over the centuries, the powerful drama he made of her story, a story of what happens when an individual person stands against the rules and the politics of the city and country she lives in, or a small powerless girl stands up to an all-powerful-seeming king, or a single person refuses to do what a tyrant says she should, has been performed and rewritten and adapted and has never lost its relevance or its vitality. It is the kind of story which will always be relevant, for all sorts of reasons, because some things never change, no matter what century we're in, and no matter where we are in history. And it is a story about what matters to human beings, and how human beings make things meaningful, how we act towards one another, and what power is, what it makes us do, and how much and how little power human beings really have.

CROW: So you are adapting this story from Sophocles' adaptation of the story in ancient mythology in turn?

ALI: Yes.

CROW: Isn't that like stealing?

ALI: No, I don't think so. It's the way most stories get told, over time. It's one of the ways stories survive.

CROW: Is it like when I swoop down on something that looks good to eat, like if there's a dead horse or some thrown-away food, and choose the best part of it and help myself, then take to the air again?

ALI: Sort of. Stories *are* a kind of nourishment. We do need them, and the fact that the story of Antigone, a story about a girl who wants to honour the body of her dead brother, and why she does, keeps being told suggests that we do need this story, that it might be one of the ways that we make life and death meaningful, that it might be a way to help us understand life and death, and that there's something nourishing in it, even though it is full of terrible and difficult things, a very dark story full of sadness.

CROW: Yes. Hmm. I've read Sophocles' version (in preparation for doing this interview with you, of course) and I'm interested to see that although you are very much adapting his version of Antigone's story, you have added some extra characters to it: I specifically mean the characters of me, the crow and the dog who sits waiting at the gate.

ALI: Yes, that's sort-of true. But only sort-of true, because—

CROW: I mean, personally I think you did this rather well, because you made me quite important, obviously, and the dog a lot less important, I mean when it comes to narrative emphasis, and this is true, isn't it? I mean it's true that crows are much more interesting and important than dogs, who tend to be rather dull and stupid. But can I just ask, why did you add us?

ALI: The thing is, Crow, the imagery in the original drama is *full* of crows and dogs. Birds and dogs are always being mentioned, because there's the question, in the original, of what happens to a body when you leave it unburied.

CROW: Delicious.

ALI: Yes, well, that's your opinion, but it's not everybody's. What I'm saying is that in the original there's this suggestion that we're nothing but carcasses, and that the wild will devour us, devour everything, unless we do something about it. And at the same time, Sophocles lets us see a special relationship between humans and creatures and something even more powerful. This happens quite late in the story, when Sophocles brings in the character of Tiresias, who is like a kind of magic priest, through whom both the natural and the spiritual worlds can express themselves, both at once, without any borders between. He can bring messages from the birds *and* the gods.

And through the whole play, the whole story of Antigone, there are questions which, though they are unspoken, are still there nonetheless, about the borders of things, the borders between animal and human and spiritual. There are questions about wildness and tameness, questions about what civilized behaviour is and what is savage, questions about what is natural and what isn't, and what is spiritual and what isn't. So it seemed to me obvious that you both were there, very present in this story, the dog and the crow, when it came to adapting something so full of questions about loyalty and nature and truth, a story about human behaviour, animal behaviour and spiritual behaviour. Animals are full of spirit too, I think.

CROW: And I have more spirit than a stupid dog, obviously, so it's only right that you chose to make me so important in the plot.

ALI: You're being a bit unfair to dogs, there. But that's the way of the world, unfortunately. It's the easiest thing in the world, to decide that someone else or something else isn't the same as us, or can be dismissed or decided about or made less than us, or made not to belong, or be excluded. It's the basis of all power struggles. It's the basis, in fact, of the story of Antigone, and all its questions about nature and human nature.

CROW: Oh, very clever, very clever.

ALI: Yes, it's a very clever story, thanks to Sophocles.

CROW: Stupid still-alives.

ALI: And stop looking at my eyes like that. They're mine.

CROW: Stupid still-alives and their oh-so clever-clever stories.

ALI: Yes, it's a wonderful story, and still very alive after nearly twenty-five centuries. Like you.

CROW: Are you calling me past it, stupid still-alive?

ALI: Quite the opposite.

CROW: Caw. Good.

THE CREATORS OF THIS BOOK

ALI SMITH was born in Inverness, where she was quite good at ice-skating and spent a lot of time on the back of a black Shetland pony called Hodrum. When she was about seven years old she began to write stories and poems. The first poem that she remembers writing was about a girl called Isabel debating with an adder, which was threatening to bite her, about which of them would live the longest. (Isabel won.)

LAURA PAOLETTI is a very young artist from Macerata, with a degree in painting. She paints, illustrates, photographs, collects birds' feathers. She has always had a mania for drawing, and even as a child she did this on walls, on trousers, on hands and the face. Selected at Bologna in 2010 for the exhibition *The Grammar of Figures*, today, with *Antigone*, she has illustrated her first book.

SAVE THE STORY is a library of favourite stories from around the world, retold for today's children by some of the best contemporary writers. The stories they retell span cultures (from Ancient Greece to nineteenth-century Russia), time and genres (from comedy and romance to mythology and the realist novel), and they have inspired all manner of artists for many generations.

Save the Story is a mission in book form: saving great stories from oblivion by retelling them for a new, younger generation.

THE SCUOLA HOLDEN (Holden School) was born in Turin in 1994. At the School one studies "storytelling", namely the secret of telling stories in all possible languages: books, cinema, television, theatre, comic strips—with extravagant results.

This series is dedicated to Achille, Aglaia, Arturo, Clara, Kostas, Olivia, Pietro, Samuele, Sandra, Sebastiano and Sofia.

PUSHKIN CHILDREN'S BOOKS

Just as we all are, children are fascinated by stories. From the earliest age, we love to hear about monsters and heroes, romance and death, disaster and rescue, from every place and time.

In 2013, we created Pushkin Children's Books to share these tales from different languages and cultures with younger readers, and to open the door to the wide, colourful worlds these stories offer.

From picture books and adventure stories to fairy tales and classics, and from fifty-year-old bestsellers to current huge successes abroad, the books on the Pushkin Children's list reflect the very best stories from around the world, for our most discerning readers of all: children.

For more great stories, visit www.pushkinchildrens.com